My Favorite BUBBLES

ROSA LINDA CRUZ

Second Edition: April 2017

Illustrated by: Alex Ray

ONE BUBBLE
TWO BUBBLES
THREE BUBBLES
MORE!

SINGLE BUBBLES
DOUBLE BUBBLES
TRIPLE BUBBLES
GALORE!

MANY BUBBLES OF MANY KINDS
SMALL, TEENY, TINY BUBBLES
BIG, GIGANTIC,
ENORMOUS
BUBBLES!

5

SHINING BUBBLES

GLISTENING BUBBLES

MESMERIZING BUBBLES!

SWERVING BUBBLES
BOUNCING BUBBLES
RUNNING
BUBBLES!

9

FALLING BUBBLES
FLYING BUBBLES
SWIMMING
BUBBLES!

TICKLING BUBBLES DANCING BUBBLES!

13

BUBBLES MAKE ME SMILE

BUBBLES MAKE ME GRIN

BUBBLES MAKE ME GIGGLE

BUBBLES MAKE ME LAUGH

BUBBLES MAKE ME

HAPPY!

15

BUBBLES MAKE ME SAY HE HE

BUBBLES MAKE ME SAY HA HA

BUBBLES MAKE ME SAY HO HO

BUBBLES GIVE ME

SO MUCH

JOY!

DO YOU LOVE BUBBLES TOO?

19

THE END!

Made in the USA
Lexington, KY
01 September 2019